Hairy Maclary, SIT

Lynley Dodd

Gareth Stevens Publishing
MILWAUKEE

Something was happening
down in the Park;
such a yap
could be heard,
such a blusterous bark.
A fidget of dogs
lined up on the grass
for the Kennel Club's
Special
Obedience
Class.

Hairy Maclary
felt breezily bad,
jittery, skittery,
mischievous,
mad.
The leader said
"SIT!"
but he wouldn't obey.
The other dogs sat,
but he scampered
away.

Galloping here,
galloping there,
rollicking,
frolicking,
EVERYWHERE.

"DOWN!"
called the leader,
so tangled in knots
that
off in a hurry
sped Bottomley Potts.

Galloping here,
galloping there,
rollicking,
frolicking,
EVERYWHERE.

"HEEL!"
cried the leader,
but
skipping away
to follow the others
went Muffin McLay.

Galloping here,
galloping there,
rollicking,
frolicking,
EVERYWHERE.

"STAY!"
roared the leader,
husky and hoarse,
but
out of his clutches
slipped Hercules Morse.

Galloping here,
galloping there,
rollicking,
frolicking,
EVERYWHERE.

"COME!"
howled the leader,
but
looking for fun
were Bitzer Maloney
and Schnitzel von Krumm.

Galloping here,
galloping there,
rollicking,
frolicking,
EVERYWHERE.

"WAIT!"
yelled the leader,
but
capering free
went Custard
and Noodle
and Barnacle B.

Galloping here,
galloping there,
rollicking,
frolicking,
EVERYWHERE.

They raced round the fountain,
they chased through the trees,
they barged over gardens
and scattered the leaves.
They hurtled past sheds
and the bandstand beyond;
they rushed through a hedge
and
went . . .

29

SPLAT
in the
pond.

Acknowledgement from Gareth Stevens:

Nearly fourteen years ago when my daughter, Loren, was two years old (and with me at the Bologna Book Fair in Italy), she demanded that I read the first Hairy Maclary story (in its original New Zealand edition) no fewer than ten times a night for the four nights of the Fair. So, I licensed the North American rights, and Lynley Dodd graciously allowed me to acknowledge in print Loren's part in convincing me to publish. Hairy Maclary from Donaldson's Dairy *and its sequels and spin-offs have since enjoyed huge success, proving Loren's exquisite taste. Now, at nearly sixteen, Loren is a delightful cross between "Daddy's angel" and all that is mischievous in Hairy Maclary. Loren:* Hairy Maclary, Sit *is for you. Love, Dad.*

For a free color catalog describing Gareth Stevens Publishing's list of high-quality books and multimedia programs, call 1-800-542-2595 (USA) or 1-800-461-9120 (Canada). Gareth Stevens Publishing's Fax: (414) 225-0377.
See our catalog, too, on the World Wide Web: http://gsinc.com

GOLD STAR FIRST READERS

A Dragon in a Wagon
The Apple Tree
Find Me a Tiger
Hairy Maclary from Donaldson's Dairy
Hairy Maclary Scattercat
Hairy Maclary, Sit
Hairy Maclary's Bone
Hairy Maclary's Caterwaul Caper
Hairy Maclary's Rumpus at the Vet

Hairy Maclary's Showbusiness
The Minister's Cat ABC
Schnitzel von Krumm Forget-Me-Not
Schnitzel von Krumm's Basketwork
Slinky Malinki
Slinky Malinki, Open the Door
The Smallest Turtle
Wake Up, Bear

Library of Congress Cataloging-in-Publication Data

Dodd, Lynley.
    Hairy Maclary, sit / by Lynley Dodd. — North American ed.
      p. cm. — (Gold star first readers)
    Summary: Mischievous Hairy Maclary finds that he is not in the mood for the Kennel Club's obedience class.
    ISBN 0-8368-2093-2 (lib. bdg.)
    [1. Dogs—Fiction. 2. Humorous stories. 3. Stories in rhyme.] I. Title. II. Series.
PZ8.3.D637Hak   1998
[E]—dc21
                                        97-35443

North American edition first published in 1998 by
Gareth Stevens Publishing
1555 North RiverCenter Drive, Suite 201
Milwaukee, Wisconsin 53212 USA

First published in 1997 in New Zealand by Mallinson Rendel Publishers Ltd., Wellington, New Zealand. Original © 1997 by Lynley Dodd.

Printed in Mexico

1 2 3 4 5 6 7 8 9 02 01 00 99 98